VICTOR SHMUD
TOTAL
EXPERT

Night of the
Living Things

VICTOR SHMUD
TOTAL EXPERT

Night of the Living Things

BOOK TWO

JIM BENTON

SCHOLASTIC INC.

Copyright © 2018 by Jim Benton

This book is being published simultaneously in hardcover by Scholastic Press.

All rights reserved. Published by Scholastic Inc., *Publishers since 1920.* SCHOLASTIC, SCHOLASTIC PRESS, and associated logos are trademarks and/or registered trademarks of Scholastic Inc.

The publisher does not have any control over and does not assume any responsibility for author or third-party websites or their content.

No part of this publication may be reproduced, stored in a retrieval system, or transmitted in any form or by any means, electronic, mechanical, photocopying, recording, or otherwise, without written permission of the publisher. For information regarding permission, write to Scholastic Inc., Attention: Permissions Department, 557 Broadway, New York, NY 10012.

This book is a work of fiction. Names, characters, places, and incidents are either the product of the author's imagination or are used fictitiously, and any resemblance to actual persons, living or dead, business establishments, events, or locales is entirely coincidental.

ISBN 978-0-545-93234-9

10 9 8 7 6 5 4 3 2 1   18 19 20 21 22

Printed in the U.S.A.   40

First printing 2018

Book design by Jim Benton

Thanks to Kristen LeClerc,
Summer Benton,
Abby McAden, Yaffa Jaskoll,
and Kerianne Okie

Nothing can keep you down.

TABLE OF CONTENTS

CHAPTER 1
WHAT TO DO. WHAT TO DO.

Victor threw another carrot at Dumpylumps and it stuck with a loud *thunk* in the wall behind him.

"It's thrilling and dangerous, but I don't think vegetable-throwing has the same sort of flash that knife-throwing does," Victor said, putting the last carrot into his pocket. "And Mom won't let me throw knives, so I don't think that this is a thing we'll be doing."

Dumpylumps offered him an ax.

"No, I'm not throwing axes at you, either," Victor said. "And you really shouldn't even have this. You could have broken it."

Victor placed the ax safely on a shelf while Dumpylumps put on a tiny cowboy hat and galloped around the room as if he were riding a horse.

"The Old West *again*?" Victor sighed. "I appreciate you helping me come up with ideas for our next thing to do, Dumpylumps, but I don't think it's possible to do a cowboy thing without a horse."

Dumpylumps handed Victor the hat and pouted.

"I know you really want to do this one, but it's just not going to work," Victor said, and he tossed the hat across the room, where it landed in a laundry basket.

"Hey! Great thinking, Dumpylumps!" Victor said. "I know just the thing that we're doing tomorrow!"

CHAPTER 2
SPORTS EQUIPMENT

Victor walked with Dumpylumps down the school hallway.

"We'll need to pick up a couple kindergartners before we go to gym class," Victor said. "Go choose a couple lively volunteers."

Dumpylumps walked into a classroom and came out with two kindergartners.

"I'll bet they have names," Victor said, patting them on their heads. "Maybe we'll find out what they are sometime."

He handed Dumpylumps some rope.

"Help me tie these children to my feet," he said.

Victor walked into gym class and his teacher, Mr. Durtburt, immediately noticed that Victor was much taller than he used to be.

"Victor. What are you wearing?" Mr. Durtburt shouted.

"It's a shirt with a big letter *V* on it. It stands for Victor."

"I mean, on your feet."

"Oh, these? These are my new basketball shoes. They're made out of kindergartners. They make me taller and I won't get as tired running up and down the court."

Victor took off dribbling the basketball while the happy kindergartners huffed and puffed beneath his feet.

"This is really a major improvement over the old kind of shoe," he shouted. "I wonder if they'd make good swim fins."

"It's against the rules!" Mr. Durtburt yelled.

"Show me where it says that," Victor said, steering the kindergartners to walk over to his teacher.

"I don't have a copy of the rules," he said.

"Good thing that I do," Victor said, and he pulled them out of his pocket and handed them to Mr. Durtburt.

"These aren't the real rules, Victor. It looks like you wrote these yourself last night."

"That's not true. I wrote them this morning. That makes them the most updated rules available. They're fresh."

BASKETBALL RULES

1. CHILDREN MAY BE WORN AS SHOES.

2. IF YOU CAN'T FIND A BASKETBALL, YOU CAN USE A PUMPKIN INSTEAD.

3. EXTRA POINTS IF YOU KIND OF DANCE WHILE YOU'RE RUNNING!

"Take those kids off your feet and return them to their classroom," Mr. Durtburt said firmly.

"Well, you're breaking the rules," Victor said. "But you're the boss."

He removed the children and gestured to Dumpylumps, who took the kindergartners by the hands.

"No worries, Mr. Durtburt. That chicken has a way with kids."

The kindergartners waved as they left.

"Good-bye, shoes," Victor called to them.

CHAPTER 3
THE NEW CHEF

Victor walked into the lunchroom and sat down next to his friend Patti.

"Hi, Patti. Dumpylumps and I are looking for our next thing. I was already a shoe designer and a professional basketball player this morning, but it turns out that the basketball leagues can be very close-minded about their rules."

Patty took a bite of her hot dog.

"I always think of you as one of the smartest people I know. I'll bet you have a thing we can do," he told her.

"Ugh." She scowled. "This hot dog is terrible. Maybe you should be in charge of the school lunches. That could be your new thing."

"It's true that I am an expert chef," Victor said. "You've probably heard of my famous dish, 'Bread with Clear Gravy.' It's spectacular."

"What's clear gravy?"

"It's water," he said in a whisper. "But please, don't share that with everybody. Since we're friends, I'll give you a copy of the recipe, but we chefs like to keep our secrets."

Dumpylumps took out his little notebook.

"Dumpylumps. Please give Patti a copy of the recipe."

Dumpylumps handed her a sheet of paper with scribbles on it.

Victor walked back into the kitchen of the cafeteria. He looked around at the people getting the food ready.

He banged a big metal spoon on a pot and spoke in a loud, firm voice.

"Which one of you is the head chef? My name is Victor Shmud and we're going to do things differently around here from now on."

CHAPTER 4
A NOTE FROM THE PRINCIPAL

Victor's mom and dad shook their heads sadly as they read the note from the principal.

"Victor, you can't just walk into the cafeteria and start telling adults what to do."

"You're wrong, Mom. That comes quite easily to me."

"Your mother means that *you're not allowed* to do it," Victor's dad said.

"Okay. I understand. No more telling adults what to do," Victor said. "And the chicken won't do it, either."

"You know that thing's a duck, right?" Victor's mom said as Victor went up to his room.

"Dumpylumps, it looks like I have to postpone my cooking career. I'm especially concerned because it's nearly bedtime and we haven't done a thing yet today. Please give me the list of things I've been telling you to write down."

Dumpylumps handed him an official memo.

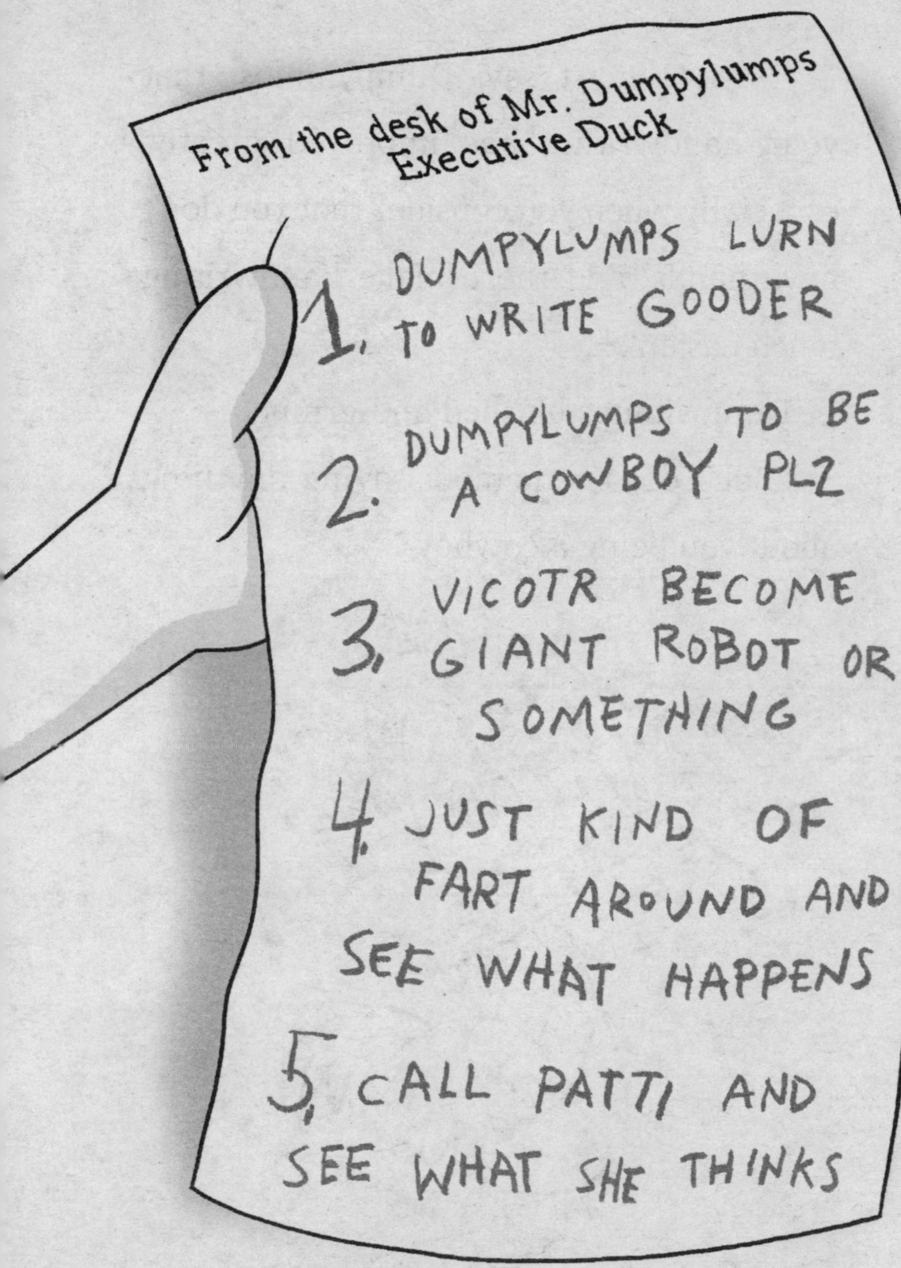
From the desk of Mr. Dumpylumps
Executive Duck
1. DUMPYLUMPS LURN TO WRITE GOODER
2. DUMPYLUMPS TO BE A COWBOY PLZ
3. VICOTR BECOME GIANT ROBOT OR SOMETHING
4. JUST KIND OF FART AROUND AND SEE WHAT HAPPENS
5. CALL PATTI AND SEE WHAT SHE THINKS

"First, I must say, Dumpylumps, that your handwriting has improved greatly, especially when you consider that you don't have hands, and those make handwriting much easier."

Dumpylumps blushed and grinned.

"But I don't remember saying anything about you being a cowboy."

Dumpylumps shrugged.

"And although I still feel that number two on the list is a terrific idea, I really like what I see going on in number four."

Dumpylumps nodded thoughtfully.

"It's not a specific thing, and it's a known fact that if you aren't making specific plans, they never fall through."

Dumpylumps handed Victor his phone. Dumpylumps had already dialed Victor's friend Patti.

"Excellent thinking. Let's begin with number five. Patti is quite brilliant about things like this. She'll have an idea."

Patti answered her phone.

"I'm so glad you called, Victor," she said. "You're rescuing me from my cello practice."

"Rescuing is one of my main things," Victor said, and he listed some of his earlier rescues.

"Remember when I saved that lady who was being eaten by a bear?"

"That was just a fur coat, Victor."

"Well, what about that time that Plumporski was attacked by a python? I saved him."

"That was a garden hose, and he wasn't happy that you cut it in half."

"And nobody will ever forget when I rescued that turtle who was being kidnapped by that bicycler."

"That was a bike helmet."

SOMETIMES I HOLD UP BUCKETS TO CATCH THE DANGEROUS ELECTRICITY THAT COULD BE LEAKING OUT OF UNUSED OUTLETS.

IT'S AMAZING HOW MANY PEOPLE JUST DON'T APPRECIATE BEING SAVED SOMETIMES.

"But, I'm saving you, right?" Victor said hopefully. "You said I'm saving you."

"Yes, Victor. You're saving me from practicing."

"Well, if you don't like the cello, why do you keep playing it?"

"I love how it sounds, but it's kind of heavy and a chore to lug around."

"Fortunately for you, I'm an instrument inventor," Victor said. "We'll have a new and improved cello ready for you tomorrow. See you in the morning, Patti. Just get to school bright and early."

Victor hung up his phone with a smile.

"Whew!" Victor huffed as he dragged Dumpylumps out of his bed. "That was close, wasn't it? We nearly went an entire day without doing a thing."

Dumpylumps pretended to smile.

"Now please bring me my box of instrument parts," he asked him. "We have important work to do."

CHAPTER 5

WELL, CELLO THERE

The next morning, Victor walked into his parents' bedroom very, very early. Neither was awake yet and his dad was snoring loudly.

He heard their alarm go off and he
watched his mom angrily slap at the clock.

He moved close and stared into her tired eyes.

"Ugh," he said. "What happened to you?"

"Nothing happened to me," she groaned. "I just woke up. I haven't even had my coffee yet. Why are you up so early?"

"This is when we instrument inventors wake up, Mom. My cellos are full of notes, and if my musicians don't get started early, they'll never be able to play them all. I just wanted to say good-bye."

After a quick breakfast, Victor's mom and dad gave him a big hug and he and Dumpylumps hurried out the front door, dragging a large bag behind them.

They made it to school swiftly and waited patiently for Patti to arrive. When she got there, Victor proudly revealed his newest creation to her.

"What do you think, Patti?" he asked, modeling the invention for her. "It's light-weight and super easy to carry, because you don't have to actually carry it at all. It's a cello that you wear."

Dumpylumps handed him the bow.

"It's really comfortable. I think I could probably climb a coconut tree in this."

"Why would you need to climb a coconut tree wearing a cello?" Patti asked.

"What kind of a tree would *you* climb to get coconuts, Patti?" Victor answered, and he began to play.

As Victor pulled the bow across the strings, it made a loud, screechy sound, like something a goat in a terrible mood might make if it sat on a cactus. And when he pushed in the other direction, it moaned like a whale with a tuba stuck in its blow-hole. Patti had never heard anything like it in her entire life.

And she wasn't the only one who heard it.

"How do you like that?" Victor asked proudly. "Pretty musical, huh? You might not believe it, but I've never had a single lesson."

"I believe it," Patti said.

"Well, this beautiful cello is yours now," he said. "I'll be looking forward to hearing you play it."

Patti smiled, hoping that she could do a little better with it than Victor had.

"I can't wait to show it to my music teacher," she said.

"Isn't that her coming now?" Victor asked.

Patti's music teacher, Miss Steinway, shuffled past them and grunted something that sounded a bit like "good morning," but not exactly.

"What happened to her?" Patti whispered.

"I've seen this before. Adults are a little slow when they wake up. If she's like my mom, she needs her coffee."

He turned to Dumpylumps.

"Please add that to my list of why adults are weird," he told him, and Dumpylumps added to the bottom of a very, very long list.

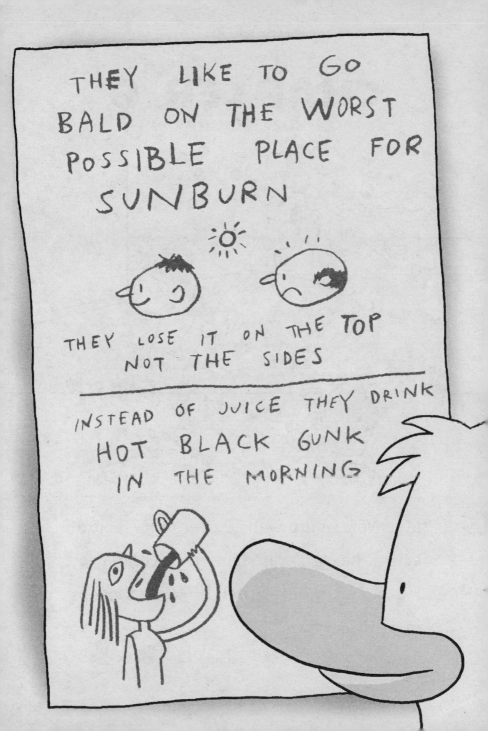

CHAPTER 6

NOZZLEBURP

SLOSH

GURSH

Mrs. Nozzleburp walked over to the board. When the class was silent, they could hear her organs sliding around like pork chops in a grocery bag.

Still, Victor considered her to be one of the most beautiful women he had ever met, and it filled him with delight when he caught the faint fragrance of one of her many prescription ointments dancing on the breeze.

He knew that he would never forget the first time he saw her. He had walked into the classroom early, and she was sitting peacefully at her desk, surrounded by a beautiful light, like you might see surrounding an angel or fairy princess.

It turned out to be some sort of therapy lamp her doctor made her sit under every day due to a skin condition, but it was still a beautiful glow, and it really brought out the watery glimmer of her weepy left eye.

"Today, we're going to be talking about the Old West," she said. "But Patti, you may be excused to go down to your music class."

Victor raised his hand.

"Mrs. Nozzleburp, I need to go with Patti. She's testing out a new cello I invented and I need to be there in case something goes wrong, like it explodes or catches us all on fire or something."

Mrs. Nozzleburp fell over flat on her face.

"I think she's fainted!" Patti said, gently patting their teacher's face. "This feels like warm dough," she said.

"I'll get a doctor!" Victor yelled, and he ran from the classroom.

Victor ran back into the classroom moments later with the janitor, Mr. Plumporski.

"Mrs. Nozzleburp fainted," Victor said. "I told her about the cello dangers and it was too much for her. It's because she loves me and worries about me so."

Mr. Plumporski examined the scene.

"If necessary, I'm willing to donate organs, of course," Victor said as he attempted to smooth out some of the wrinkles in Mrs. Nozzleburp's unconscious face.

"Don't let the shriveling alarm you, Mr. Plumporski," Victor said. "That's kind of her look."

"Are you sure she didn't just slip on something?" Mr. Plumporski asked.

Then Mrs. Nozzleburp spoke in a weak voice, which was very surprising because nobody thought her voice could get any weaker.

"I tripped on a duck," she said as she wobbled back up onto her feet.

"We'll be on the lookout for one," Victor said as he pushed Patti out of the room. "So happy you're all right. We need to go to music class now."

"It was probably Dumpylumps," Patti whispered to him.

"Dumpylumps is a chicken. Are you saying that our teacher can't tell a duck from a chicken? A mistake like that is the kind of thing that gets teachers fired, and that's a pretty mean thing to do, Patti."

They stopped by her locker and picked up the cello Victor had made her.

CHAPTER 7
DIG THIS MUSIC

Victor helped Patti into her cello just as Dumpylumps walked in with a bandage on his head and cowboy boots on his feet.

"Where was he?" Patti asked.

"Dumpylumps is interested in the Old West. He wants to try being a cowboy one day, and I like to encourage his dreams. I think he stayed back to hear what Mrs. Nozzleburp had to say about it."

"That's probably when she tripped over him," Patti said.

"Patti," said Victor. "Please listen more carefully. Mrs. Nozzleburp said she tripped over a *duck,* not a chicken.

"And please stop trying to get that glorious princess into trouble by accusing her of not knowing the difference," Victor said as he pulled a smaller instrument out of a bag and put it on Dumpylumps.

"Look! I made a violin as well!"

Miss Steinway stood quietly in the corner. She drank her coffee as she waited patiently to hear these new instruments.

Patti set up her sheet music and Dumpylumps studied it carefully. He swatted at it a couple of times.

"I told you before. Those are notes, not bugs. Just play them," Victor said. "And play them well."

Patti and Dumpylumps pulled their bows across the strings and created a sound even more horrible than before. They looked hopefully at Miss Steinway, but she didn't seem pleased.

In fact, the noise had made her accidentally take a large bite out of her coffee cup.

"I don't think that was exactly what you were going for," she said.

"I couldn't agree more," Victor added.

"Let me just get rid of this broken cup and I'll be right back to talk about this."

"Yes, there's clearly a problem here," Victor said.

Miss Steinway closed the door behind her.

"The problem is that they need to be MUCH louder," Victor said, and he dragged microphones in front of the instruments. He turned the volume up as far as it would go.

"Try it again," he said, and then waved his hands like a conductor as they pulled the bows across the strings.

The terrible sound wave tore through the school and rattled every window. It scared Miss Steinway so much she took another bite out of a new coffee cup.

Mr. Plumporski's mustache fell off and Mrs. Nozzleburp's loose neck skin flapped like a flag in heavy winds.

The sound echoed far beyond the school and shook the headstones in the graveyard.

Twisted hands clawed the grass from underneath the soil, and zombies dragged themselves up through the wet dirt.

The horrific music of Victor's instruments had awakened them and they began stumbling slowly in the direction of the school.

Mud and worms fell from their decaying faces as they gnashed their teeth and moaned horribly.

"That was beautiful," Victor said.

CHAPTER 8

ANOTHER NOTE

Victor's mom and dad shook their heads sadly as they read ANOTHER note from the principal.

"Victor, these instruments you made created a lot of trouble today."

"Mom, not everybody appreciates fine music."

"It says here that parts of Mrs. Nozzleburp were still flapping at the end of the day," Dad said. "What do you have to say to that?"

"*Flapping* makes it sound unattractive, Dad. Say *fluttering*. Fluttering. It sounds more like a butterfly that way."

"You can't take instruments you make to school again, Victor," his mom said.

"Okay, Mom," Victor agreed.

"And they want you to go in early and put them in your locker. They said they'll leave them outside the office door."

"I'll do it, Mom," he said. Then he kissed them both and carried Dumpylumps up to his room.

"I guess we did a thing today," Victor said. "We knocked a mustache right off a janitor with a cello. That's a thing."

Dumpylumps shrugged, unimpressed.

"You're right. That's not very remarkable. Probably happens every day. Maybe tomorrow we can do something more unusual. Please make a note of that."

Dumpylumps turned from the window to write in his little notebook, and while he did, he didn't notice the crowd of zombies shambling past their house.

CHAPTER 9
GETTING A BITE WITH
AN OLD FRIEND

The next morning, Victor and Dumpylumps
walked to school very early.

"I want to get those instruments back before I get into any more trouble," Victor said. "And if we're lucky, maybe we'll find Mr. Plumporski's mustache. There's probably enough there for us to share, if we both want a mustache."

They walked along the empty, quiet street.

"It's still dark," Victor said. "Maybe we'll see birds and squirrels asleep on the grass."

Dumpylumps looked around nervously. Victor could tell he was scared.

"Don't be afraid of the dark. There's absolutely nothing out here to worry about," Victor said, and he patted Dumpylumps on the head and calmed him down. Then a zombie leaped from behind a bush and grabbed them.

"HOT BANANAS!" Victor shouted as he jerked himself free from the zombie, who clung tightly to Dumpylumps.

"Leave him alone! He's just a helpless chicken!" Victor shouted, and he remembered that he still had a carrot in his pocket. He threw it as hard as he could and it bounced right off the zombie's forehead.

The stunned creature dropped Dumpylumps, and he and Victor ran as fast as they could. When they were a block ahead of the zombie, they stopped and looked back.

"I guess vegetables really are good for your health," Victor said.

The zombie quickly recovered from the carrot attack and continued shuffling toward them slowly, moaning horribly.

Then, joining him from the left and right, more zombies emerged from the darkness, groaning and growling as they hobbled along.

"I don't know how many zombies you need for a zombie invasion, but this seems like it should be enough," Victor said.

Dumpylumps tugged insistently on Victor's shirt.

"No need to panic. Look how slow they are," Victor said. "We can easily beat them to the school if we run."

CHAPTER 10
BACK AT SCHOOL

"We need a plan," Victor said. "The zombies will be here any minute."

They ran and picked up the bag of instruments by the office, then paused in the lobby of the school to catch their breath.

The buses were beginning to arrive and kids were already beginning to stroll into the school.

Dumpylumps scribbled something on his sheet of paper and showed it to Victor.

HEY ZOMBIES EAT THE OTHER KIDS NOT US

"Excellent handwriting," Victor said, "but we want to save *all* of the kids."

Dumpylumps wrote something on the other side and held it up.

"That's better," Victor said. "But not quite right. This type of flirting could lead to dating, and you don't want to rush into marriage with a zombie, do you?"

Dumpylumps thought for a moment and shook his head *no*.

"I guess I should probably reveal to you now that I am an Expert Zombie Fighter," Victor announced.

Patti walked in and waved to them.

"Hey, guys," she said. "What's up?"

Before they could answer, Patti saw for herself as dozens of zombies poured through the door into the school.

"To the cafeteria!" Victor yelled, and they took off in a run as their classmates screamed and scrambled away from the zombies.

"The cafeteria! Perfect!" Patti said. "We can hide from them there."

"Hide from them? I'm going to make them follow us there!"

They burst into the cafeteria kitchen and Victor put on an apron, hairnet, and gloves.

"Remember, Patti? I'm an expert chef."

Victor looked around at the people getting the food ready.

He banged a big metal spoon on a pot and spoke in a loud, firm voice.

"I'm not allowed to tell you what to do, but I can tell you this: The school has been invaded by zombies, and we're all going to do something to attract them here."

"I cook better alone, anyway," Victor
said.

Victor took a couple of packages from the refrigerator and stuck them in the microwave.

"I don't know what brains taste like, but I'm pretty sure they smell like cafeteria hot dogs," Victor said. "And I'm sure that's what these zombies are after."

He prepared them on a plate and set them down on a table. Then he opened the door for all the zombies to rush in.

"Come and get it!" he shouted into the hallway.

But no zombies were there.

He could hear their groans coming from other parts of the school, but no zombies came for the hot dogs.

"I should have realized. I'm too good of a chef," Victor said. "I've prepared these hot dogs so well that zombies aren't interested in them anymore."

Victor opened the big bag and told Patti and Dumpylumps to put on the instruments.

"These might help protect you from zombie bites," he said. "We're going to have to hunt them down."

They walked cautiously through the halls, moving in the direction of the zombie groans.

"Those moans sound somehow . . . familiar," Victor whispered.

They peeked carefully around a corner and saw the zombies clawing at the door to the teachers' lounge.

"Of course!" Victor said quietly. "Teachers have the biggest brains of all. The teachers must be hiding in there and the zombies can smell their sweet, delicious, bulging brains. I think every once in a while, I even catch a whiff of them."

"What are we going to do?" Patti whispered.

"We're going to back out of here very quietly," Victor said, "and call somebody for help." As they were backing up, Patti's bow got tangled in Dumpylumps's violin strings.

And it made THE NOISE.

CHAPTER 11
SYMPHONY OF DISASTER

THE NOISE! The terrible noise! The zombies whirled around and stared at them with their buggy, bloodshot eyes. They began frantically waving their arms and groaning.

"Run!" Patti yelled, and they took off down the hallway.

With every step, the bow dragged across the strings. The faster they ran, the louder it became, and the louder the zombies groaned.

Victor looked back at their angry, empty faces and their dark, tired eyes.

"They just look so familiar to me," he said.

They dashed around a corner and ran into the library.

"Protect yourselves!" Victor shouted. "I have an idea!"

And then he ran out of the library, leaving Patti and Dumpylumps alone with the zombies.

"*This* was his idea? Abandoning us with the zombies?"

Dumpylumps thought it was probably a pretty good idea. He would have done it if he had thought of it first.

The two of them began piling up books and tables between themselves and the zombies, with their instrument suits making horrible noises the entire time.

Victor ran down the hall, looking in every classroom.

"Not here," he said, and went to the next one.

"Nope."

Finally he opened one and smiled broadly.

"Ah HAH!" he said. "There you are. I hope you know exactly what you must do."

The zombies couldn't reach Patti and Dumpylumps past the books and stuff they had piled up. Patti struggled with her cello suit.

"Quick! While we have a minute, let's take these things off!" she said.

Suddenly the library door flew open.

Victor looked quite heroic as he stood dramatically in a strong breeze.

"I stopped for a moment to set up some lights and a fan before I came in. Do I look heroic?" he asked.

"HELP US!" Patti shrieked.

"Hey, zombies!" he yelled. "I know what you want."

He put his hands on his hips.

"Patti, Dumpylumps," he commanded. "Smash those instruments!"

Patti and Dumpylumps smashed the instruments, and the zombies smiled for the first time.

"They weren't attracted to the sound," Victor said. "They HATED the sound!"

The kindergartners tied to Victor's feet reared up on their hind legs and Victor yelled like a cowboy.

"Yeeee-haw!"

The kindergartners whinnied like horses and galloped in a circle around the zombies.

"Why are you wearing kindergartners?" Patti yelled.

"They make it harder for the zombies to reach me," Victor said.

"But isn't it dangerous for the kindergartners?"

"Look at those little heads. They don't have big brains yet. The zombies aren't very interested in them."

"And a few more wanted to help, too," Victor said, and when he whistled, three more kindergartners charged into the library.

Patti quickly tied hers to her feet, and Dumpylumps rode his like a horse.

"Patti, keep saying smart things. I need the zombies to know how fat and ripe your brain is."

"The capital of Germany is Berlin!" Patti yelled, and they took off out of the library with the zombies running after them.

They skidded around a corner and crashed into Mr. Plumporski, the janitor.

As he tried to get to his feet, a couple of the zombies started heading toward him.

Victor grabbed Mr. Plumporski's thermos.

"Patti! More brain stuff!" He shouted.

"An elephant can hold two gallons of water in its trunk," Patti yelled. The zombies turned their attention back toward her and they took off down the hall again.

"What's the plan?" Patti yelled to Victor. "It seems like we're just running in circles."

"That's exactly what we're doing," Victor said. "I thought you two were enjoying this."

"No! Get on with it! Let's end this!" she shouted, and Victor made a fast right turn.

"Down this hallway!" he yelled. "Follow me!"

He stopped in front of the teachers' lounge.

"This is what they *really* want," he said.

"We're going to let them eat the teachers?" Patti asked.

Dumpylumps thought this was a great idea. He nodded and gave a thumbs-up.

"Doesn't that seem wrong?" Patti asked.

"A little," Victor said, and he pushed open the door.

CHAPTER 12

CREAM AND SUGAR

"They like brains, of course, because they're zombies. But that's not what they want the most," Victor said.

The zombies stumbled past them into the room, grinning broadly.

"They want coffee," Victor said.

"Coffee?" Patti said.

Dumpylumps began pouring cup after cup for the zombies, who smiled and sat down next to the teachers to drink it.

"They weren't attracted to the sound of the cellos. They HATED it. And they hated it because that sound is what woke them up. You ever see an adult slap at an alarm clock? There's no sound in the entire world that they hate more than whatever sound wakes them up."

A zombie raised his cup in thanks at Victor.

"But now they're up. And there's one thing adults need more than anything when they get up—coffee. That's why they were clawing at the teachers' lounge. They could smell the coffee inside."

"That's why you thought they looked familiar."

"That's right, they reminded me of my mom."

"I think it's best that you never tell her that," Patti said.

"Don't you think it would make her happy to know that she had helped save the day?" Victor asked.

"No," Patti said. "Not. At. All."

CHAPTER 13
GARGGH GARGH GLARGH

Mrs. Nozzleburp's desk was empty.

"Where's the teacher?" Patti asked.

"We have a substitute today," Victor said.

"Mrs. Nozzleburp is getting a little rest today. She still hasn't fully recovered from that fainting spell of hers."

"I'm pretty sure she tripped on Dumpylumps," Patti said.

The door opened and the substitute walked in and wrote her name on the board.

"Miss Urhhhgh Urgh?" Patti said, reading the name. The substitute turned and smiled at her.

"Garggh gargh glargh," she said.

"It's a zombie!" Patti said nervously.

"They make great substitutes," Victor said. "They work for the coffee, and they're very interested in making our brains bigger."

"But I can't understand a word she's saying."

"That's okay," Victor said. "Nobody really listens to the substitutes anyway."

Later that evening, Dumpylumps was taking notes from Victor.

"I think we can officially call what we did today a thing," Victor said. "You can add Shoemaker, Zombie Hunter, Janitor Shaver, Expert Chef, Cello Maker, and Guy Who Hires the Substitute Teachers to my list of things."

Dumpylumps scribbled some words that looked quite a lot like what Victor had just said.

Then Dumpylumps put on his cowboy hat, climbed up onto his kindergartner, and began riding him around the room.

"You can't just keep him, you know," Victor said. "You don't own him."

"My parents know I'm here for a play-date, Mr. Victor," the kindergartner said.

"Oh. In that case, have fun," Victor said, and he watched as Dumpylumps rode into the sunset on the back of his noble five-year-old stallion.

Actually, it was just a lamp that he had set up to make it look like a sunset.